For Hera, Fionn, Ruth, Tadhg and Maia, master storytellers all - S.C.

Farshore

First published in Great Britain 2019 by Farshore
This edition published in Great Britain 2021 by Dean

An imprint of HarperCollinsPublishers
1 London Bridge Street, London SE1 9GF
www.farshorebooks.com

HarperCollinsPublishers
1st Floor, Watermarque Building, Ringsend Road, Dublin 4, Ireland

Text copyright © Sarah Coyle 2019
Illustrations copyright © Dan Taylor 2019
Sarah Coyle and Dan Taylor have asserted their moral rights.

ISBN 978 0 6035 8080 2
Printed in China
1

A CIP catalogue record for this title is available from the British Library.

Farshore takes its responsibility to the planet and its inhabitants very seriously.
We aim to use papers from well-managed forests run by responsible suppliers.

THE BIGGEST STORY

SARAH COYLE

DAN TAYLOR

Farshore

Errol's mum told the **best stories**. They were always fun and exciting. So one afternoon, when there was nothing to do, Errol knew a story was just what he needed.

Unfortunately, there was a plumbing problem.

"Sorry, Errol," said his mum. "This pipe won't fix itself.
Why don't **YOU** think up a story instead?"

Errol blinked, surprised.
Then he shook his head.

"I can't tell a story.

I don't know how."

"Bet you can,"
said his mum.
"Just have a go."

Out in the garden, Errol tried hard to think of a story. But star jumps didn't shake any ideas out.

And staying upside down for a full minute only made his ears hurt.

He was so busy thinking, he didn't notice the ants until . . .

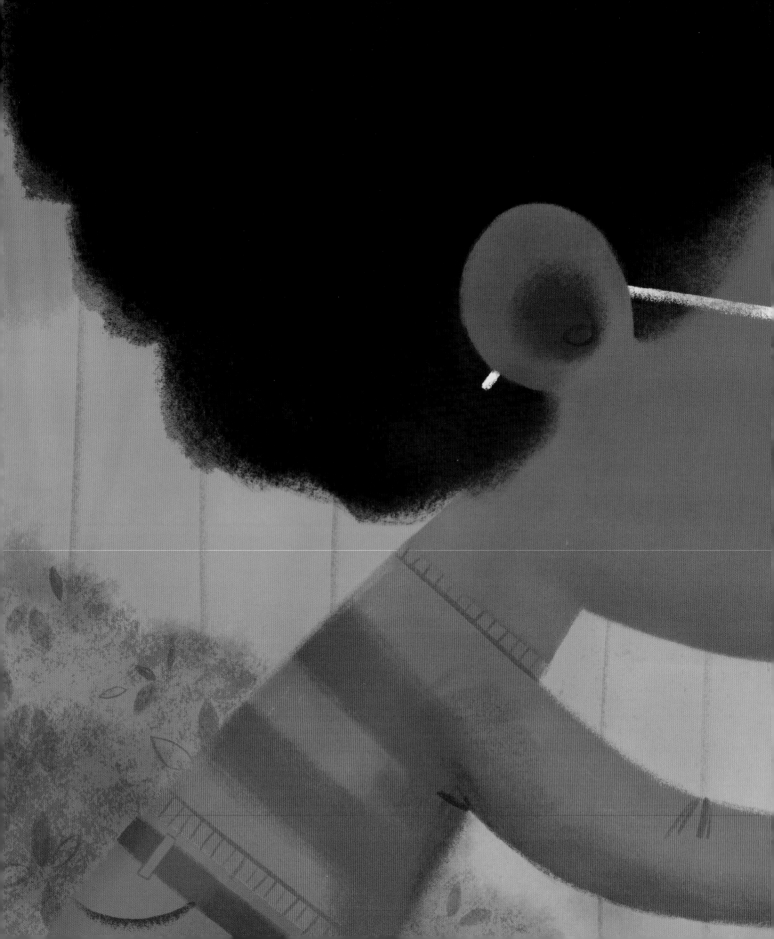

"Pssssst!"
said the biggest ant.
"We couldn't help
overhearing that
you're telling a story.
Will it have ants in it?"

"Uh . . .
WOW, sure,"
said Errol.
He'd never met
a talking ant
before. Perhaps
other animals
could talk?

"Ahem . . ."
said a low voice.

A tabby cat was tapping Errol's foot.
"You know . . ." she said. "The best
stories have **cats** in them."

With an awful kerfuffle, all the neighbourhood cats
bobbed up onto the fence. Each cat sat at a polite
distance from others. Cats like a bit of space.

"So, what do you say?" asked a tortoiseshell cat.
"Any room for cats in your story?"

Ants and cats! Errol's story was getting better already.

"Hmmm," Errol looked round the garden. "What else does my story need?"

"Stunts!"

shouted a sheep, clipping the gate
as she jumped into the garden.
Showering splinters, a long line of
sheep hopped after her.

"You need **action!**
Excitement!
Paragliding!

Sheep do all that stuff."

"Done," Errol grinned. He had everything he needed to start his story.

But just then . . .

. . . the ground trembled and shook. A mob of meerkats
burst through the fence. Elephants, lizards, pandas,
monkeys, even a sleek leopard, followed.

"So . . ." the leopard looked excited. "Word in
the wildlife park is you're telling a story.
Good news! We're in!"

Errol gave a low whistle. To fit everyone in, this story would have to be **big**. "Okay," he said. "But that's definitely it. There's no room for anyone else. Not even . . ."

"DINOSAURS!"
shouted the sheep.

A Stegosaurus and a gigantic T. rex stood,
beaming, as they sank slowly into the lawn.
"A new story is always worth travelling through
time and space for," the T. rex explained.

"'Course, we were in the very first stories,"

said the Stegosaurus, smugly.

"Hope this one is as good . . ."

The audience fell silent, waiting for the story to begin.
Errol gulped. He felt as though he had eaten
too much pizza . . . and the pizza was made of bees.

Would his story be any good?

"I've got my tea!" Errol's mum sat down, but didn't seem to notice that her chair was covered in monkeys. "I'm all ready for your story!"

Errol grinned at her. Then he took a deep breath and began . . .

THE BIGGEST STORY

OH NO! T. REX IS IN TROUBLE! SHE'S STUCK IN THE MIDDLE OF...

THOSE TRICKSY CATS HAVE TRAPPED HER!

BUT HERE COME T. REX'S FRIENDS! HOORAY!

POOR T.REX! NOT EVEN HER FRIENDS CAN HELP HER NOW.

S THIS THE END FOR T.REX?!

WAIT! IS IT? NO, IT CAN'T BE...

"The End!" said Errol.

Seconds stretched . . .

then the audience went . . .

WILD!

Animals cheered, roared and stomped.

Dinosaurs danced, ants somersaulted,
cats purred louder than lawnmowers and
sheep ping-ponged across the lawn.

Errol's mum pulled him into a huge hug.

"That was the best and the biggest story I've ever heard!" she cried. "Much better than any of mine."

Tired but happy, Errol went upstairs for his bath.
He felt very proud. He had told his own story
and his head was full of ideas for more.

A little later, Errol's boat was sailing past bubbled mountains, when he heard a tiny tap-tap-tapping.

A small owl stuck her head through the open window, "Did I miss the story?"

"Yup," said Errol. Crossing the dangerous bath-water deeps, the boat began to rock. "But I'll tell you another.

It starts on a stormy sea . . ."

Errol had lots of fun making up his story. If you told a story, what would it be about? After a few star jumps, try out this idea to get started.

Choose a Name

....

....

....

and the

Sticky

Magical

Giant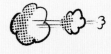

Funny

Speedy

Incredible

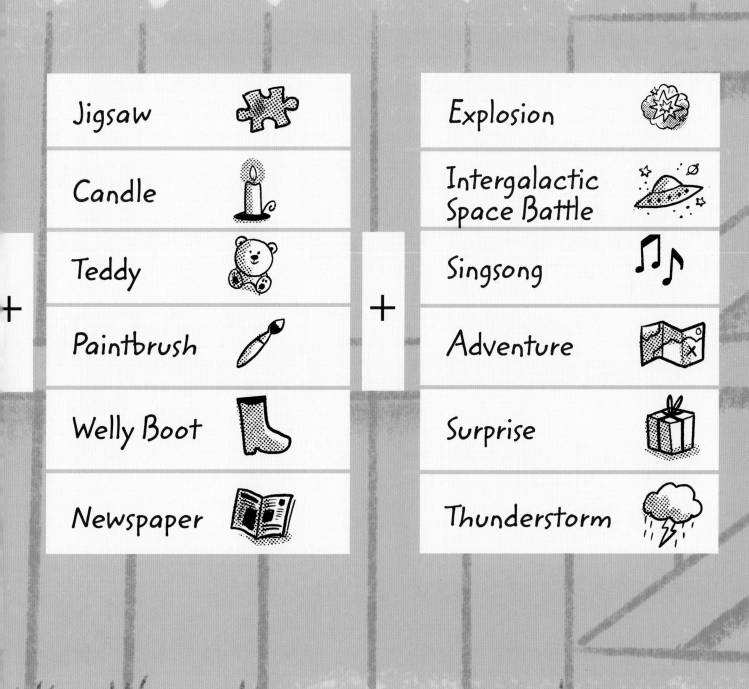

+

Jigsaw	
Candle	
Teddy	
Paintbrush	
Welly Boot	
Newspaper	

+

Explosion	
Intergalactic Space Battle	
Singsong	
Adventure	
Surprise	
Thunderstorm